Holidays Amaze

Karen Petit

WESTBOW
PRESS®
A DIVISION OF THOMAS NELSON
& ZONDERVAN

This is a work of fiction. All of the characters, names, incidents, organizations, and dialogue in this novel are either the products of the author's imagination or are used fictitiously.

WestBow Press books may be ordered through booksellers or by contacting:

WestBow Press
A Division of Thomas Nelson & Zondervan
1663 Liberty Drive
Bloomington, IN 47403
www.westbowpress.com
1 (866) 928-1240

ISBN: 978-1-9736-3685-4 (sc)
ISBN: 978-1-9736-3684-7 (hc)
ISBN: 978-1-9736-3686-1 (e)

Library of Congress Control Number: 2018909727

Print information available on the last page.

WestBow Press rev. date: 08/21/2018

Contents

Preface

Are holidays a maze, or do holidays amaze? With different kinds of poetry, *Holidays Amaze* shows that holidays are both. Whether a maze is difficult or incredibly fascinating to traverse, the freedom to choose from different paths is amazing! Family activities, meetings with friends, religious services, smiles from strangers, and other positive experiences are all incredible pathways to follow for amazing holidays.

Like mazes and poetry, holidays are structured in a variety of forms, including federal, state, religious, vacation, personal, and family dates of celebration. People can even "speak holiday," which is defined by the *Oxford English Dictionary* as "to use choice language, different from that of ordinary life," as seen in Shakespeare's *Merry Wives of Windsor:* "He writes verses, hee speakes holliday, he smels April and May."[1]

Holidays Amaze has twenty-eight poems with content connected to different holidays and celebrations. Because of the large number of holidays, only some of the most important ones are referenced in the poetic content of this book. However, many of the themes and symbols in *Holidays Amaze* are components of all holidays and celebrations.

The poetry in *Holidays Amaze* includes maze poems, prayer poems, traditional sonnets, and narratives. The three maze poems have the word "maze" in their titles. The prayer poems include the word "prayer" in their titles. The traditional sonnets can be spotted through their structures, such as Iambic Pentameter rhythm in Shakespearean sonnets. The narrative poems in *Holidays Amaze* have historic elements, dream/reality content, dialogue, and other creative components. For example, in the "Waiting in Advent" poem, different rhythms are used for dialogue spoken by different characters.

Before Dr. Karen Petit (www.drkarenpetit.com) wrote *Holidays Amaze,* the theme of following different paths had been included by many authors in many works of literature. One of many illustrations exists in Robert Frost's poem, "The Road Not Taken." Two roads are referenced: "Two roads diverged in a wood."[2] Whenever we have the choice of choosing from more than one road or path, our lives become more interesting. We do not need to just follow a single road, especially if it has a lot of traffic on it. We often choose to drive on the one "less travelled by,"[3] just like Frost chose in his poem "The Road Not Taken."

Mazes have different paths that people can choose, so maze poems can give readers more freedom in their choices. The maze poems in *Holidays Amaze* are followed by traditionally formatted versions of the same maze poems, so readers can enjoy the maze version, as well as the traditional version, of each one. "A Maze Poem: A Maze of Choices for New Year's Day" has different possible orders for some of the stanzas. A traditional version of this poem, "A Maze of Choices for New Year's Day," has the words typed in stanzas, rather than in boxes inside of mazes. The traditional stanza version only has one possible order shown; however, multiple logical arrangements are visible in the boxes of the maze-poem version. To partially connect together the content of "A Maze Poem: A Maze of Choices For New Year's Day" and "A Maze of Choices For New Year's Day," both the maze and the traditional versions of these poems include the following sentence more than once: "Raising the next page will amass more maze."

A poem can be an amazing maze, whether it is formatted like a maze, an image, lines in stanzas, or other ways. Poetry of any format can be amazing because of its creative structure, images, and use of sound to enhance the content for an exciting reading experience. The creative structures can include sentences, grammatical elements, organization, format, design, and multimodal components. Images are often "seen" in the metaphors, similes, symbolic elements, format, sentence structures, use of icons, and the structure of a poem. Aural elements are hearable through the rhythms, rhymes, alliteration, and other sound elements. Poetry is thus multimodal, which is why it is so much fun to read.

Reading poetry on a holiday can be especially amazing as one of the positive activities of the day. Because of the large number of endeavors and the desire to make loved ones happy, holidays are truly amazing mazes. With family, friends, and our many blessings, *Holidays Amaze!*

Acknowledgements

My loving family has been amazingly supportive throughout my whole life. My thanks go to my children (Chris and Cathy), to my brothers and sisters (Ray, Rick, Margaret, Carl, Sam, Bill, Dan, and Anne), and to my nieces, nephews, cousins, and other relatives. I especially love meeting with my family on the holidays.

My thanks are extended to my many friends and colleagues at Phillips Memorial Baptist Church, the Community College of Rhode Island, Bristol Community College, Bryant University, Massasoit Community College, New England Institute of Technology, Quinsigamond Community College, Rhode Island College, Roger Williams University, the University of Massachusetts at Dartmouth, the University of Rhode Island, Worcester State University, and the Association of Rhode Island Authors.

I also thank WestBow Press for the wonderful support they have given to me and to many other Christian authors. Historically and today, publishers have been expanding the knowledge and literacy skills of our world.

I am most thankful to Jesus Christ, my Lord and Savior, for his sacrificial, amazing, and loving help. God's miracles for me and other people in our world are so many, and the Holy Spirit's presence is one of these miracles. With His help, the maze of my life has become an amazing life.

Illustrations

A Maze Poem: Mazes on Holidays

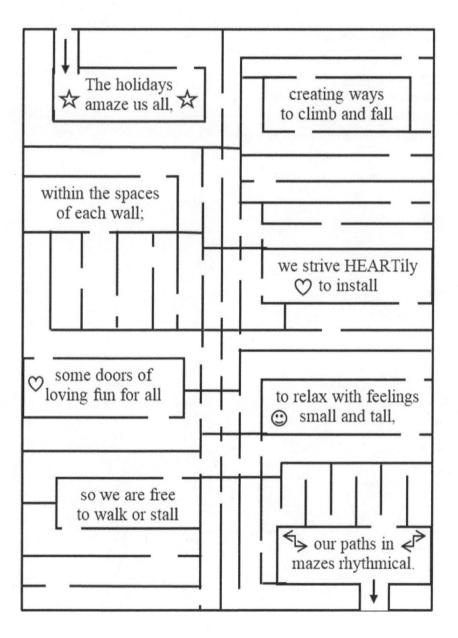

The holidays ☆ amaze us all, ☆

creating ways to climb and fall

within the spaces of each wall;

we strive HEARTily ♡ to install

♡ some doors of loving fun for all

to relax with feelings ☺ small and tall,

so we are free to walk or stall

our paths in mazes rhythmical.

Mazes on Holidays

The holidays amaze us all,
creating ways to climb and fall
within the spaces of each wall;
we strive HEARTily to install
our doors of loving fun for all
to relax with feelings small and tall,
so we are free to walk or stall
our paths in mazes rhythmical.

A Maze Poem: A Maze of Choices for New Year's Day

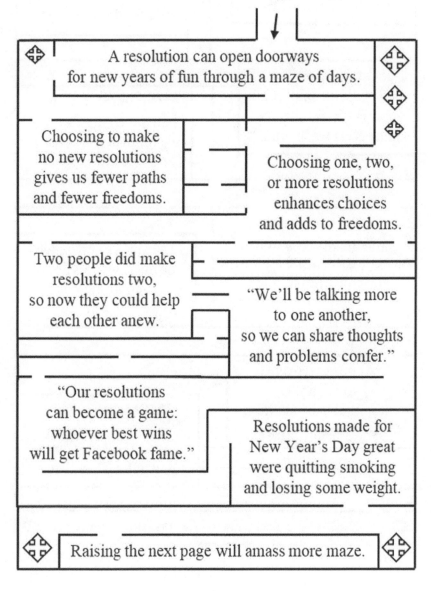

A resolution can open doorways
for new years of fun through a maze of days.

Choosing to make
no new resolutions
gives us fewer paths
and fewer freedoms.

Choosing one, two,
or more resolutions
enhances choices
and adds to freedoms.

Two people did make
resolutions two,
so now they could help
each other anew.

"We'll be talking more
to one another,
so we can share thoughts
and problems confer."

"Our resolutions
can become a game:
whoever best wins
will get Facebook fame."

Resolutions made for
New Year's Day great
were quitting smoking
and losing some weight.

Raising the next page will amass more maze.

"Last night in a dream,
our ovens appeared.
One was smoking, and
one was fat and weird."

"Our ovens must have
needed to lose weight
and to quit smoking;
cold food is not great."

"Our toaster oven
just kept on smoking;
it was too dangerous
and a great trash thing."

"Our microwave fat
had not enough space;
we thought it was trash
and would it replace."

"The toaster oven
was smoking so much;
we coughed while it burned
and could not it touch."

"The smoke surrounded
the microwave's nook,
hiding its big door,
so we could not cook."

"At our two ovens,
I so did holler:
'Stop that bad smoking!
Make yourself smaller!'"

"The toaster oven
and the microwave
both did yell back at me
'bout habits they crave."

Raising the next page will amass more maze.

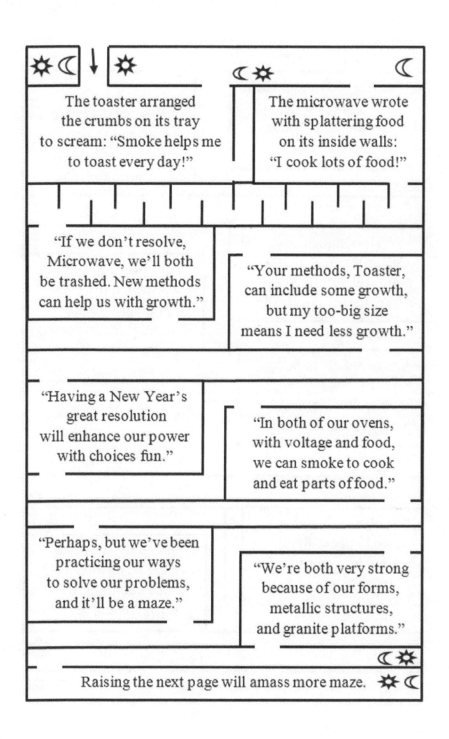

The toaster arranged the crumbs on its tray to scream: "Smoke helps me to toast every day!"

The microwave wrote with splattering food on its inside walls: "I cook lots of food!"

"If we don't resolve, Microwave, we'll both be trashed. New methods can help us with growth."

"Your methods, Toaster, can include some growth, but my too-big size means I need less growth."

"Having a New Year's great resolution will enhance our power with choices fun."

"In both of our ovens, with voltage and food, we can smoke to cook and eat parts of food."

"Perhaps, but we've been practicing our ways to solve our problems, and it'll be a maze."

"We're both very strong because of our forms, metallic structures, and granite platforms."

Raising the next page will amass more maze.

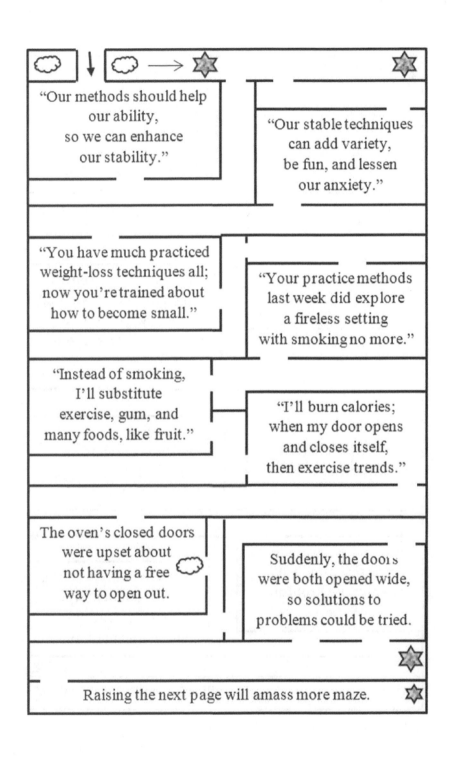

"Our methods should help
our ability,
so we can enhance
our stability."

"Our stable techniques
can add variety,
be fun, and lessen
our anxiety."

"You have much practiced
weight-loss techniques all;
now you're trained about
how to become small."

"Your practice methods
last week did explore
a fireless setting
with smoking no more."

"Instead of smoking,
I'll substitute
exercise, gum, and
many foods, like fruit."

"I'll burn calories;
when my door opens
and closes itself,
then exercise trends."

The oven's closed doors
were upset about
not having a free
way to open out.

Suddenly, the doors
were both opened wide,
so solutions to
problems could be tried.

Raising the next page will amass more maze.

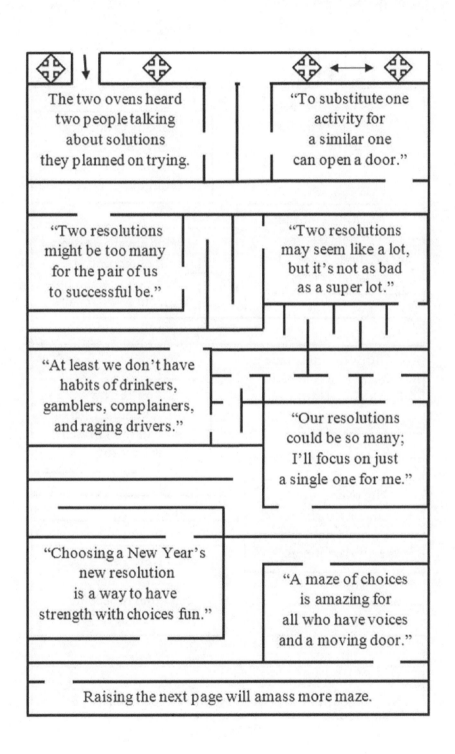

The two ovens heard
two people talking
about solutions
they planned on trying.

"To substitute one
activity for
a similar one
can open a door."

"Two resolutions
might be too many
for the pair of us
to successful be."

"Two resolutions
may seem like a lot,
but it's not as bad
as a super lot."

"At least we don't have
habits of drinkers,
gamblers, complainers,
and raging drivers."

"Our resolutions
could be so many;
I'll focus on just
a single one for me."

"Choosing a New Year's
new resolution
is a way to have
strength with choices fun."

"A maze of choices
is amazing for
all who have voices
and a moving door."

Raising the next page will amass more maze.

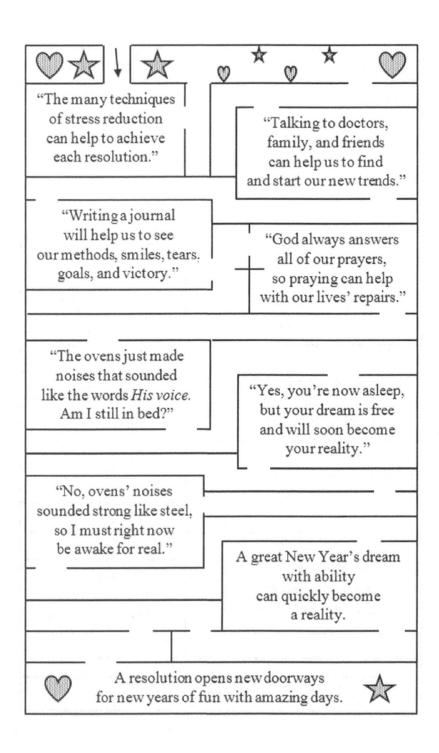

"The many techniques
of stress reduction
can help to achieve
each resolution."

"Talking to doctors,
family, and friends
can help us to find
and start our new trends."

"Writing a journal
will help us to see
our methods, smiles, tears,
goals, and victory."

"God always answers
all of our prayers,
so praying can help
with our lives' repairs."

"The ovens just made
noises that sounded
like the words *His voice*.
Am I still in bed?"

"Yes, you're now asleep,
but your dream is free
and will soon become
your reality."

"No, ovens' noises
sounded strong like steel,
so I must right now
be awake for real."

A great New Year's dream
with ability
can quickly become
a reality.

A resolution opens new doorways
for new years of fun with amazing days.

A Maze of Choices for New Year's Day

A resolution can open doorways
for new years of fun through a maze of days.

Choosing to make no new resolutions
gives us fewer paths and fewer freedoms.

Choosing one, two, or more resolutions
enhances choices and adds to freedoms.

Two people (*+) did make resolutions two,
so now they could help each other anew.

*"We'll be talking more to one another,
so we can share thoughts and problems confer."

+"Our resolutions can become a game:
whoever best wins will get Facebook fame."

Resolutions made for New Year's Day great
were quitting smoking and losing some weight.

Raising the next page will amass more maze.

*"Last night in a dream, our ovens appeared.
One was smoking, and one was fat and weird."

+"Our ovens must have needed to lose weight
and to quit smoking; cold food is not great."

*"Our toaster oven just kept on smoking;
it was too dangerous and a great trash thing."

*"Our microwave fat had not enough space;
we thought it was trash and would it replace."

*"The toaster oven was smoking so much;
we coughed while it burned and could not it touch."

*"The smoke surrounded the microwave's nook,
hiding its big door, so we could not cook."

*"At our two ovens, I so did holler:
'Stop that bad smoking! Make yourself smaller!'"

*"The toaster oven (<) and the microwave (>)
both did yell back at me 'bout habits they crave."

Raising the next page will amass more maze.

<The toaster arranged the crumbs on its tray
to scream: "Smoke helps me to toast every day!"

>The microwave wrote with splattering food
on its inside walls: "I cook lots of food!"

<"If we don't resolve, Microwave, we'll both
be trashed. New methods can help us with growth."

>"Your methods, Toaster, can include some growth,
but my too-big size means I need less growth."

<"Having a New Year's great resolution
will enhance our power with choices fun."

>"In both of our ovens, with voltage and food,
we can smoke to cook and eat parts of food."

<"Perhaps, but we've been practicing our ways
to solve our problems, and it'll be a maze."

>"We're both very strong because of our forms,
metallic structures, and granite platforms."

Raising the next page will amass more maze.

<"Our methods should help our ability,
so we can enhance our stability."

>"Our stable techniques can add variety,
be fun, and lessen our anxiety."

<"You have much practiced weight-loss techniques all;
now you're trained about how to become small."

>"Your practice methods last week did explore
a fireless setting with smoking no more."

<"Instead of smoking, I'll substitute
exercise, gum, and many foods, like fruit."

>"I'll burn calories; when my door opens
and closes itself, then exercise trends."

The oven's closed doors were upset about
not having a free way to open out.

Suddenly, the doors were both opened wide,
so solutions to problems could be tried.

Raising the next page will amass more maze.

The two ovens heard two people talking
about solutions they planned on trying.

+"To substitute one activity for
a similar one can open a door."

*"Two resolutions might be too many
for the pair of us to successful be."

+"Two resolutions may seem like a lot,
but it's not as bad as a super lot."

*"At least we don't have habits of drinkers,
gamblers, complainers, and raging drivers."

+"Our resolutions could be so many;
I'll focus on just a single one for me."

*"Choosing a New Year's new resolution
is a way to have strength with choices fun."

+"A maze of choices is amazing for
all who have voices and a moving door."

Raising the next page will amass more maze.

*"The many techniques of stress reduction
can help to achieve each resolution."

+"Talking to doctors, family, and friends
can help us to find and start our new trends."

*"Writing a journal will help us to see
our methods, smiles, tears, goals, and victory."

+"God always answers all of our prayers,
so praying can help with our lives' repairs."

*"The ovens just made noises that sounded
like the words *His voice.* Am I still in bed?"

+"Yes, you're now asleep, but your dream is free
and will soon become your reality."

*"No, ovens' noises sounded strong like steel,
so I must right now be awake for real."

A great New Year's dream with ability
can quickly become a reality.

A resolution opens new doorways
for new years of fun with amazing days.

Intermixing Coffee on Martin Luther King, Jr. Day

The cupboard's back space had black coffee cups:
on hooks the cups were all hanging sadly
in spots like slaves with no chance of hookups
to some freedom of shifting forward, free.

The cupboard's front space had coffee cups white:
on wooden ground were they all standing straight
with no hooks to keep them in spots unbright;
at times, they'd even roll from cupboard's gate.

"I love Martin Luther King Junior's speech,
'I Have a Dream.' He would never have placed
his coffee cups like this." A hand did reach
and make the black and white cups interlaced.

Like people on buses, the cups became free
to intermix and taste of each other's coffee.

Lovers' Retreat Bridge in Roger Williams
Park, Providence, Rhode Island

Love Branches on Valentine's Day

Two limbs of trees at Lovers' Retreat Bridge
in Roger Williams Park both want to join
their tips and create a new, higher bridge
that will their two wooden branches conjoin.

The reaching trees are on opposite sides
of the bridge; their tips are inches apart.
With breezes blowing, each of their limbs slides
back and forth, waving "hi" from a high heart.

The branches speak through the sounds of wind controlled
and tell each other their names: Jess and Miles.
They're wanting to spring warm from winter cold;
their branches spin sunward with matching smiles.

A skinny squirrel climbs up Jess's trunk.
Its eyes stare hungrily at Jess's bark.
With wind's support, Miles drives a tasty chunk
of bark across the road, on Jess to park.

The squirrel eats the bark from Miles and waves
a "thank you" while jumping down to the ground.
The squirrel turns in circles and behaves
like a bird as it keeps dancing around.

Some red cardinals land on Miles and Jess.
Like the squirrel on the ground, the birds dance
in circular rhythms. They then progress
to reach their nests: treehouses for romance.

While all of the nests seem nearly complete,
the birds still find more twigs and bits of plants;
to one another, they're helpful and sweet
while finishing nests with supporting plants.

Waving their highest limbs into the wind,
Miles and Jess break some of their own twigs small
and let them fall down with the gusting wind
to the cardinals building nests not tall.

The birds raise the twigs, wave their wings of growth,
thank the trees, and quickly finish each nest.
The trees enjoy these outer rings of growth
as circles great within their stems suggest.

The newest rings within the wooden stems
of Miles and Jess join the stems' older rings
to mimic the forms of circular gems
and create an idea for wedding rings.

The wind increases, causing birds to sing.
The closest limbs of Jess and Miles connect
and dance together as a sparkling ring
of bark is blown from Miles to Jess bedeck.

The wet engagement ring is shining from
snowflakes and stays on one of Jess's limbs.
More snow falls onto Jess and her loved one,
so dressed for a wedding are all their limbs.

The birds do sing as Miles and Jess exchange rings.
Their limbs become forever connected
across the bridge, and now their inner rings
are outer rings on branches intersected.

Walking below the branches connected
by Miles and Jess are two humans married,

who are from the cold and wind protected
by branches of trees slowing the wind's speed.

The humans look at the touching branches.
The female says, "These trees are feeding us
our air. Even with no leaves on branches,
oxygen's still being produced for us."

Rubbing his wedding ring on his wife's ring,
the male says, "You're so right. Trees use water
and carbon dioxide while they're making
glucose; oxygen emissions occur."

With music playing from some singing birds,
the married couple smiles, hugs, and dances;
they share their loving ideas with their words
about connecting to nearby branches:

"We should breathe closer to branches to share
our carbon dioxide with every tree
that has branches needing parts of our air
to make our oxygen for us for free."

"We should grow more branches, just like the trees."
"We'll then be branchers with limbs covered in bark
to give to others with every breeze."
"We can even give money to this park."

"More branching people are needed to feed
our church and other nonprofits with love."
"If branches of trees can help those in need,
human branchers, too, should branch out their love."

On the bridge, the two humans kiss anew.
The trees, too, press their touching limbs closer;
they too are sharing kisses. Two by two,
the warmth of love melts the snow of winter.

With help from God, the rings of branching love
spin water from snow into chemistry,
which connects to soil, roots, stems, and air above,
to create and preserve biology.

The strength of love branches outward to give,
so branchers can breathe, relate, love, and live.

Thankful for Presidents on Presidents Day

A president first in our nation anew
with later leaders helped our lives to accrue
from different backgrounds to be unified
into United States, built with steps to stride
through and beyond political parties
to create our nation of voters to please
with freedom and thankfulness for pioneers
like Washington and Lincoln for many years.

Sticking Together on Easter

Twelve children were set for an Easter egg hunt:
hugging each bag brightened on the back and front
with pictures proclaiming the Easter story
of their Lord and Savior's loving glory:
an empty cross and tomb were brightened by light
flowing from God for humanity's delight.

The youngest child moved forward his right leg
and tried to pick up the closest plastic egg,
but his brother said, "Your leg's wrong not to wait
for other children to quickly navigate
around the pond with its new water lilies
that shelter the fish, so they feel at ease
when people's shadows upon the water walk
near the fish and make noises as they talk."

The girl who was nearest the pond turned around,
faced the brothers, and asked, "Can't people be drowned
if they walk on water, or were you speaking
of people walking near water and seeking
paths where they'd walk on dry ground while their shadows
would walk on the water with no wet clothes?"

"My words were unclear shadows, meaning shadows
of people above the pond's watery woes
with plenty of steps upon the pond's surface,
but people and fish are kept safe with God's grace."

The girl said, "Jesus, not just his shadow,
could really walk on water to places go;

He also helped Peter to walk on water
in a storm that tried to Peter's faith deter."

The youngest child showed a picture on his sock:
Jesus was helping Peter to water-walk;
the child then pulled from his bag a book to show
the hands of Jesus working miracles aglow:
many acts of feeding, healing, and helping,
such as saving the scared Peter from drowning.

Another child then asked about Peter:
"Was he one of the twelve apostles who were
called to follow Jesus, our Lord and Savior?"

"Yes, and to follow Jesus, he did prefer,
rather than remain with fishermen who were
never able to walk on waves of water."

From beyond the pond arrived some more children,
who lined up, so all were ready to begin.
The hunt for Easter eggs quickly began
after one of the teachers explained the plan
for the youngest children to be first to start,
followed by older groups who'd wait to take part.

The young child with images on his socks moved;
near his leg, he saw an egg, which he removed
from between two small hills of sandy dirt
that had made the egg seem hidden in a desert.

Attached to the egg was a sticker for lent
with a picture of Jesus, praying while bent
on his knees in the sand of the Judaean desert
with a happy heart showing his soul unhurt.

A teacher said, "That sticker shows our Lord's insights
while fasting for forty days and forty nights

to love us all and help our lives to straighten
and not curve into the temptations of Satan."

The older brother stated, "This sticker's sand
reminds me of the Lenten season's homeland,
and I understand the need to fast and pray,
for forty days beginning on Ash Wednesday."

The young child brushed some bits of sand sticking to
the egg in his hand before looking anew
and warmly opening the egg to see inside
many stickers like the one on the egg's outside.

The child removed all the stickers from inside
the egg, looked at his friends, and then did decide
to give everyone standing nearest to him
one of the stickers while he did hear a hymn,
"Christ the Lord Is Risen Today," being played
on a phone and sung by friends who nearby stayed.

All eyes looked at the next egg to be opened;
another young child, with help from her best friend,
had found an egg on a bush's branch resting.
The child pulled out from the egg a tiny ring
with a cross in the center section engraved.
A second ring inside the egg was found and saved
from being ignored by the child's helpful friend,
who talked about friendship rings to her best friend.

The child and friend each put on one of the rings,
hugged each other, and waved around their rings
to show more friends they were friends forever more
who loved and worshipped Jesus, their Lord and Savior.

Other children looked at eggs aligned nearby
on branches of bushes not terribly high;
these eggs had stickers of Jesus washing feet,

which happened directly before He did eat
the Last Supper with disciples at His sides.
The children perceived the twelve stickers were guides
to the eggs containing similar prizes
for many blessings of Easter surprises.

Twelve of the children at once the eggs gathered;
some noises from eggs being opened were heard
with sounds of twelve voices their joy to confer
followed by children looking together
at prizes similar in twelve of the eggs:
tiny finger puppets in each of the eggs
appeared to be disciples who together
had bread and wine at Jesus's Last Supper.

One child slowly lifted his finger puppet,
which was a small fisherman holding a net,
and asked his friends, "Is this a disciple?
I'm hoping it's neither Thomas nor Judas."

The oldest child said, "I don't know what they looked like,
but I would never be happy to act like
one of those two disciples. With the many
miracles Jesus did, how could someone be
a doubting Thomas, and how could anyone
who knew Jesus doubt His resurrection?"

Another child said, "I dislike Thomas, too,
but the worst of the two was the thief: Judas.
He never fit in correctly with the others;
many were fishermen, and some were brothers."

The child with the raised hand threw into the pond
his finger puppet, which skipped quickly beyond
the reach of all of his friends' extended hands
and fell into the wet water's commands.

One of the child's friends moved her hands together
and prayed: "Dear Lord, I know that wasn't Judas,
who probably wasn't a fisherman. Please,
I know you can rescue that puppet with ease."

The child with the still-raised hand was sad with tears
falling from his eyes while he said to his peers:
"Oops! That puppet probably was not Judas
because it's now standing on water like Peter;
with this breeze, it's beginning to walk on water
and looks even more like the disciple Peter."

Another child said, "We all at times mess up;
even if we don't want to be anything at all like another Judas,
we all make mistakes. Even Peter messed up.
To take away our sins, Jesus died on the cross;
if we ask for forgiveness, our sins God will toss."

The puppet on water walking suddenly
leaped high into the air with strong wind to be
fluttered back into the same child's hands reaching
out with his praying fingers, God-worshipping.

The child smiled as his fingers hugged his puppet;
even though its whole surface was very wet,
the child's fingers were showing his happiness
with their praying shape and tender caress.

Another egg was opened with the brightness
of a golden cross on a golden chain to bless
its wearer with the weight of a much smaller
cross than the one Jesus did carry taller.

The girl who had opened the egg was smiling
as she moved the cross necklace like a big ring
around her neck with the cross landing near her heart;
the girl and cross would never be torn apart.

"Here's another egg," a voice did say with glee
while picking up an egg from under a tree.
With happy hands, the girl added glad details
to the egg via the cross stickers on her nails.

All eyes stared at this next egg to be opened.
Cross stickers were stuck on each fingertip's end;
all ten crosses worked to twist the egg open,
so friends could see an Easter surprise again.

While being opened by stickered fingernails,
the egg was making clicking noises, like nails
of metal trying to connect, while inside,
to the finger's nails moving on the shell's outside.

The egg, when opened by the stickered fingernails,
revealed twelve dimes for its inside details;
the girl removed the dimes and gave them all
to friends; her nails did then within the egg crawl.

A teacher smiled. "I love those eggs being found,
and I love how you're sharing the gifts around,
but did anyone yet the best egg get,
the one containing the Jesus statuette?"

The children all looked around, shook their heads "no,"
and widened their eyes, showing they didn't know
where to start looking for such a great surprise
and how to be even more Easter-egg wise.

"The egg's between two stones, so you might assume
it's resting in a tiny version of a tomb,
like where Jesus was placed after he died
on the cross to save people He loved worldwide."

After a few seconds of children looking
around and between rocks, a child was pulling

apart two stones to view an egg with many
outer-shell stickers showing pictures plenty.

The stickers displayed Jesus's birth, childhood,
baptism, disciples, miracles all good,
Last Supper, death on the cross, resurrection,
and joining His Father: heaven ascension.
The child opened the egg without twisting it,
saw a small statue of Jesus being lit
with the sun's brightness and the smiles of his friends,
who knew their love through Jesus always extends.

Peeling off stickers from the egg's outer shell,
the child was giving them away when one fell;
he knelt downward, retrieved the fallen sticker,
and remained kneeling while being much quicker
to give stickers to his classmates happy,
who showed their stickers to each other with glee.

The kneeling child then placed one of the eggshells
on a large stone while saying, "Jesus excels
because He was raised to God from His tombstone."
The shell atop the stone looked like a throne
when the child did set the Jesus statuette
on the shell's circular form by God pre-set.

With the statuette standing up from the stone,
the image of a risen Jesus out-shown
all other items as His feet with success
stood straight and strong upon the egg's roundness.

Once all the children had some Jesus stickers,
the kneeling child stood up and stuck two stickers
on his own hands, then shook his hands with others,
which caused his stickered hands to stick to others.
A circle of children and teachers did form
around the Jesus statue with prayers so warm

that they melted moisture within the stickers,
creating dampness falling down from the stickers
to the ground and forming a tiny pond
where Christian friends with each other could bond
to join with Jesus stickers from Easter eggs
to walk on circular ponds with stable legs.

A Prayer Poem on the National Day of Prayer

Dear Lord,
On this amazing first Thursday in May,
we ask for Your help in hearing our needs
and thank You for Your miraculous deeds
as we progress forward each single day
and enjoy Your help in whatever way
You feel is appropriate for us all;
in this worldly maze with doors at each wall,
we love sublime days like today to pray.

Whenever we're stuck by a closed-door wall,
You're always so loving and forgiving;
You carve us new doors through which we can crawl
without any pieces of walls falling;
while Your hands and feet are blessing us all,
we stay on our knees to love You for giving.

In Jesus' name we pray,
Amen

Shaping Pancakes on Mother's Day

The son and daughter both awoke
early together on Mother's Day
to prepare a breakfast to evoke
their love onto their mom in May.

Brewing coffee without delay,
the son then helped the daughter to make
a breakfast in a creative way:
flower shapes for every pancake.

Smelling pancakes, their mom did wake
and walk with dad into the room,
where more than one flowered pancake
was waiting for mom's smile to bloom.

Each pancake the mom did consume
with her smile blossoming even more,
for every flower's love did zoom
between her lips, kissing for more.

The children and dad did adore
and eat some pancakes very warm
before asking mom to look for more:
a heart within a flower's form.

The mom thought the pancakes uniform,
but chose the one that was beside
the stove, warm and ready to reward
the hearts of folks with mom by their side.

The children knew their mom had eyed
the correct pancake near the stove's heat;
they smiled with admiration and pride
while moving the pancake to mom's seat.

She knew this pancake not to eat,
but instead opened it like a gift
and found inside a necklace sweet
with a heart shining to be lift.

Mom lifted the heart and then did shift
her lips apart, so she could kiss
the sweetness of the heart and lift
the sugar for her taste buds' bliss.

Extra-heart mom did hug and kiss,
so all of their hearts were joined in bliss.

A Prayer Poem on Memorial Day

Dear Lord, we're thankful on Memorial Day,
for this moment with memories to pray
within a free, usually peaceful land
for those whose service helped others to stand
and kneel on solid ground to safely stay
and remember lives in our country grand.

We love each image of a memory
of a service member being a part
of our lives 'til serving the military
did climax in death, a Purple Heart,
the respect of the people in our country,
and an afterlife in Your hands to start.

We pray for Your continued loving support
for those who have lost service men and women
as we travel through the maze of life so short
and know You will help us to find our way, then
and now, with Your strong and loving transport
to eternity when starting the end. Amen.

Rhyming on Father's Day

The third Sunday of June anew,
a daughter and a son had been
preparing for a barbecue;
the grill was now set up to begin.

The daughter had a bow-shaped pin
attached onto her blouse's collar
as she looked with a happy grin
at her brother being up to par.

He said, "That pin on your collar
so nicely matches the bowtie
that I'm wearing on my collar;
both bows our dad for us did buy."

His sister said, "The reason why
he bought them both at one time
was his love for us. He did try
to give us matching bows to rhyme."

"That rhyming idea's very nice.
That's something that we'll tell dad about."
"You've again said the word 'that' thrice.
Today's not the time to make our dad shout."

Glancing at his watch to see the time,
he smiled while placing some chicken
and steak on the grill at the same time
their parents appeared, hunger-stricken.

Staring at the steak and chicken,
the father said, "It's so nice to see
you're both working so hard again
to cook food and make me happy."

His son said, "You taught us, dad, to be
great at cooking barbecued food,
so that—
oops—I meant to just say 'so,'
so the members of our family
would all have a happy lunch mood."

The daughter laughed. "You've even booed
at us, dad, whenever we've said
any four-letter words, which are lewd,
like 'that,' so you've helped us to be led."

The children their parents then fed
while hugging and thanking their dad
for his years of having them be led
with rhymes, so their lives would both be clad.

Many great dads make children glad
with rhyming tasks they're asked to add.

The Lights of Freedom on Independence Day

On the Fourth of July, Jean fell asleep
while humming "God Bless America" to leap
into a dream about the lights of freedom
in our past, present, and future to come.

Flames of fire flickered in the dreamy sky,
working to create many lights to fly
and show the formation of freedoms great
that would to the American dream relate.

Atop a tipi fell shining rays of lights,
revealing indigenous peoples' rights;
these Natives were first on American land,
and often did help new neighbors unplanned,
like colonists strong who were trying to please
themselves and others in diverse countries.

Another flaming light lit up the sky:
a shooting ray to find Roanoke did try,
but the ray was lost before it touched the ground,
so it relit and jumped to Jamestown,
which did become the first English colony
to survive and begin the New World's glee.

A firework flashed into a circle shape,
twirling to a city-on-a-hill's landscape,
flying to its own religious landing place
in the Plymouth Rock Canopy Building's space,
and diving through an enclosure to land

on Plymouth Rock: a Pilgrim symbol grand.

The beaming light transferred itself to bounce
forward in time to view and then announce
its love for statues of founding fathers;
the National Monument to the Forefathers
had light on its structure, becoming even brighter
where the statue of Faith stood in the center.

Built to honor the Pilgrims, this monument
had a Bradford quote, bright at this segment:
"[L]ight here kindled hath shone unto many,
yea in some sort to our whole nation,"[4] and we
do see with these fireworks how our country
was brightly formed; its founders have made us free.

Bouncing back to the past, lights formed words and swirled
on Plymouth Rock: "You are the light of the world.
A city built on a hill cannot be hid" (Matt. 5:14 NRSV).
The words brightened and to other cities slid.

Another fireworks exploded and did stand
for religious freedom in Rhode Island,
where it split up into multiple rays
that landed on diverse churches to amaze
others about Roger Williams's legacy:
he believed each soul should have liberty.

Light flew to a visitor-center locale:
the Roger Williams National Memorial;
inside was a Roger Williams statue
standing next to a flag—red, white, and blue;
the proximity of these portrayals
of our freedom suggests they're all symbols
of different freedoms' integration
into the U.S. and its constitution.

Waking the dreamer was a caller unknown
who was demanding tax money on the phone:
"Your money must be sent again and again
to pay for people's taxes in Great Britain."

"You scammer! You can't demand taxes from me!
I don't live, work, shop, or vote in your country!"
The dreamer turned off the phone, went back to sleep,
and dreamed of watching with each flaming leap
a new historic freedom for a unified team
of New-World seekers of the American dream.

A growling sound emanated from a light
that lit up the sky and seemed much too bright;
the fired light split up while flaming angrily
and spread Stamp-Act protests to states many.
Fireworks lit up the Stamp Act Congress to still
make unity in the New World visible,
despite the need for quiet secrecy
of the newly-formed Sons of Liberty.

They did patriotic actions many,
like the burning of the HMS Gaspee;
they also tossed chests of tea into the sea
to claim their rights at the Boston Tea Party.

Within the dreamer's dream were sent strong-breeze
fireworks from New World colonies
that were flaming at England without fun:
"No taxation without representation."

The Declaration of Independence
in 1776 was immense
in its expression of our need to be free
while at war with Great Britain and unfree.

The American Revolution happened
with angry fireworks that did not end
until 1783
when thirteen colonies from England were free.

While writing the U.S. Constitution
beneath the fireworks of resolution,
contributors to the American dream
did help to create our freedoms that beam.

In the dream appeared Thomas Jefferson;
his initial and the revised version
of the Declaration of Independence
were displayed for the dreamer's thoughts intense.

Different contributors to our freedom
appeared in the dream to hate unfreedom;
they told the dreamer to continue to be
a helpful contributor to our country.

Washington, Lincoln, and others many
visited the dreamer who wanted to see
amazing contributors large or small
because our world's mazes need helpers all.

More fireworks were launched with explosive outcomes,
sending lights to fire up the many freedoms
accrued through speeches, debates, protests, wars,
and new constitutional amendment doors.

Watching the times and places for fireworks,
the dreamer knew the United States works
by uniting past, present, and future
donors into its maze of freedom pure
to help maintain and advance many roads
with free choices for heavy and light loads.
Our freedoms light up the American dream,

so we can all work, play, fly, drive, or stream
across the mazes of life with lit-up fun
to land at our chosen destination.

Whether in Bristol, Portsmouth, New York City,
Philadelphia, or Washington, D.C.,
our collaborative efforts can enhance
our lives with the lighted rays of freedom's stance.

Fireworks on Independence Day

A Fireworks Circle on Independence Day

Top of the Hill Overlooking Plymouth Rock
Canopy Building, Plymouth, Massachusetts

Plymouth Rock, Plymouth, Massachusetts

The National Monument to the Forefathers, Plymouth, Massachusetts

Roger Williams Statue in the Visitor Center
of the Roger Williams National Memorial, Providence, Rhode Island

Freedom to Worship God[5]

Our Lord's so strong, he really could
Just pick us up and make us act
Like perfect people being good
In settings broken or intact.

Instead, we're free to choose our acts
And free to run on different tracks.
At times, our choices may be wrong,
But prayerful hearts will help us learn
The better paths, both short and long.

Our Lord and Savior's loving grace
Erases sin and helps us turn
Our feet to run a peaceful track.
If souls and love to Jesus race,
Our ties to Him will stay intact.

The Work of Appliances on Labor Day

The washer and dryer were both too loud.
Their noisy turns expressed desire to rest
on Labor Day when many workers proud
received a holiday for rest and fest.

The top-loading washer was turning clothes
and water in horizontal circles.
The dryer had a vent, instead of a hose,
and turned its heat in vertical circles.

The dryer's venting was loud in its way
of trying to speak to others and say,
"We really should only work hard today
with double the pay of a normal day."

The washer sad was turning and splashing
its tears of water over the clothing
in its tub while it sounded like saying,
"We're still doing double our daily thing."

With their tools, noises, and actions, quickly
the washer and dryer both contacted
their one union rep: electricity;
the house's power was soon extracted.
All the appliances were now happy
for their holiday newly enacted.

The house's owners were upset and yelled
for "help" into a phone while contacting
an electrical company that held

fast to its policy of first helping
those who called first, rather than those who yelled
the most about an electrical thing.

After two hours, electricians appeared
with tools and wires to help them do their work.
At first, the washer and dryer appeared
uncertain about doing any work
until the electricity appeared
with extra juice to pay for extra work.

The washer and dryer both understood
the joy of resting on a holiday,
but they were now happier workers good
and working for extra pay on Labor Day.

Timely Road Space on World Animal Day

A carrier with bars enclosed each pet
on a trip in a van to visit the vet;
two cats in cages on second-row seats
joined two third-row dogs in staring at streets.

When the car did bump into a pothole,
the cages' doors were pushed by pets with a goal:
to open the doors and be first to run
fast to their owners for comforting fun.

Crying cats and begging dogs did implore
their owners to slow the car even more,
despite the noisy line of cars tailgating
to voice their need to get somewhere with zing.

Their van moved faster while radios blaring
from the stream of tailgating cars was scaring
the two cats into making their cries louder,
forcing more sounds of road rage to occur.

"Could that pothole have hurt our pets at all?"

"We were going slow, and it was too small."

"Even so, our pets are here; you must go slow."

"The drivers behind us need to faster go."

"They just think more time for more tasks will make each day glad."

"They think we're stealing their time, so they're really getting mad."

"They want to claim the whole entire road, not just their own space."

"More lanes in this road would mean fewer reasons to race."

"Everyone likes to have more time and a larger place."

"Less time does mean less space."

"That's why all of our pets like their own space."

"These strange drivers all want their own road space."

"Our pets are better than a speeding stranger."

"If our car's hit, won't our pets be in danger?"

"The seatbelts grasping the carriers will work."

"You're right; I'll slow down without even a smirk."

With a smirking grin, the driver slowly
decreased the speed of the van from just twenty
to ten in a forty zone, and with a frown,
did then move to the lane for cars broken down.

The cats and dogs were still trying to express
their desire for more love, slow speed, and less stress;
most of the cars were speeding while driving past
the van that would not travel very fast.

One passing car had a passenger who saw
the four loving pets, each with a paw
pushing at the inside of a cage's door
to attain more space and owner rapport.

The passenger smiled and made a hand gesture
with an extended thumb and two fingers pure
that were saying "I love you" to people, pets,
and everyone looking for visits with vets.

The slower driver gestured back with a smile,
waved at the car to pass, and for the next mile,
lowered the van's speed even more to keep
the stress of the pets from becoming too deep.

The sound of a police car's siren did reign,
forcing the van to stop in the breakdown lane;
the four loving pets turned their blinking wild eyes
toward the blue car's blinking lights and siren cries.

After seeing the pets trying to be free
and seeing why the van had moved so slowly,
the officer wrote no ticket and was quick
to direct the slow van back into traffic.

In transit, the owners to their pets did talk;
the pets stared at their voices and tried to walk
out toward their owners, but the bars of each door
did block their journeys to escape and explore.

When the van arrived late at the vet's building,
the two owners so quickly did inside bring
their pets for shots, exams, and grooming prefers,
which their pets did bear with barks and nervous purrs.

After two hours of loving care for their pets,
the people with four animals left the vet's
and started their journey to return home
with healthy cats and dogs that wanted to roam.
While driving near a peaceful field and a cop,
the slow-moving van had to briefly stop,
since other vehicles were braking there

to avoid hitting a family of deer.

Because the deer were peering at the road,
the traffic needed directions to be slowed,
so the officer was keeping safe the deer
by waving at the cars and vans that were near.

"Everyone's now careful to drive slowly;
even the deer seem shocked at slowness to see."

"If more people had seen our animals four,
they would have tolerated our slowness more."

"When you were driving in the breakdown lane,
so they could pass, extra time they did gain."

"At least one driver appeared very happy
and understood our need to drive slowly."

"While we're now moving again, we both need
to think some more about our measure of speed."

"Being free to move quickly or slowly
happens when open roads let drivers be free."

When deer ran into the road to traffic see,
the slow cars and van did stop completely;
the pets in the van kept watching the deer
while pressing on their doors to outside be near.

"Keeping cats and dogs caged up makes me sad
when deer are free to run around and be glad."

"A cop is telling those deer what to do
even though they're not caged up in a zoo."

"Some animals must love the safety of zoos

with no worries about their food to lose."

"With pausing traffic enclosing those deer,
they're partially caged, like a zoo's over here."

"Again, we're now moving the same speed slow
that we were driving a little while ago."

"Back then, by choice, we wanted to drive this slow;
we're now unhappily slow and unfree to go."

A car stopped with a wide-open window
and tied up the traffic already slow;
food from the open window then ejected,
and the pausing group of deer gladly was fed.

When the traffic moved forward, but slowly,
the deer stayed still, wanting more food to see,
while looking at the van's people and pets
with eyes begging for food and other assets.

The deer closest to the van suddenly stared
at the cage enclosing one of the cats scared;
the deer then ran with two fawns not at ease
into the field to hide behind some trees.

"Those deer smelled food before their run did begin,
but they'll find some food in the field they're now in."

"That mother was helping her fawns to stay free;
the three of them are such a dear family."

Most of the traffic was soon quickly moving,
but the van was still slow, due to wanting
to be slow enough to make the pets happy
while travelling on the road to be home free.

Turning down a street with no cars to be
leading slowly or tailgating quickly,
the van was free to drive as fast or as slow
as the people and pets wanted to go.

When arriving home, the pets were uncaged,
and no longer acted like they were road-raged,
but rather showed their need for freedom raging
as they let their love for their own space spring.

The cats were free to choose each favorite spot
inside their home to eat, purr, and play a lot
before they paused in their fast activities
to stare with love at their owners with ease.

The dogs ate food in the house to fun begin
before running into the yard fenced-in,
chasing toys with speed, playing with each owner
and enjoying the space that each did prefer.

The pets were not upset at being barred
from leaving a spacious house and fenced-in yard,
for all of life has only so much space,
and timely spots can race to stay in place.

Two Happy Dogs: a Poodle/Papillon Mix and a Purebred Papillon

One Talking Flamepoint Siamese with One Resting Flamepoint Siamese

A Deer Family

Unblocked Writing on the National Day on Writing

Pen and Pencil had been standing straight all night long
in a confining pencil holder very strong
right next to a computer, keyboard, and printer;
Pen and Pencil were dreaming of sleep to enter,
but a lady came near them with paper in hand
and then reached for their holder with an anxious hand.

The moving hand did cause a slight draft in the air.
Pen and Pencil shifted in their holder to flare
their shiny metal parts at one another's smirk;
both felt 'twas the other's turn to stay late at work.

The lady's eyes weren't even watching as her hand
hit the holder, sending Pen and Pencil to land
on each other to fight for peaceful desktop space
to support their freedom to sleep in a workplace.

As Pen and Pencil into one another rolled,
they moved atop a paper into a threshold
of writer's block: they needed the ability
to write a sleepy message to a tense lady.

When Pen and Pencil stared down at the products of trees
(blank paper and wooden desk), the tree items with ease
stared blankly up at them. Pencil's thoughts did link wooden;
it tried to write some words, but failed. It then hit Pen,
trying to make him write for the lady "Anything,"
but Pen's ink refused to flow, resulting in nothing.

Pen and Pencil were yelled at by a now-mad lady:
"Tell yourself to write something bad; you'll then feel free
to say diverse things while using methods many
to brainstorm, free write, and draft your ideas to see
what your newly uncaged thoughts may want to say freely
before you revise, edit, enhance, or vary."

Pen and Pencil hit and tried to edit each other,
resulting in compared ideas that were made to blur
before they were even written on wood or paper;
their greatest ideas were then not free to appear.

Pen rolled the strongest atop the wooden desktop,
kicked Pencil with its metal point, and made Pencil stop
its own journey toward the desk's middle section.
Pen appeared to have won, but it had no words won.

"To revise and edit thoughts unwritten partially
scares the creative ideas, causing some to flee,
resulting in no words being able to ski
with warmth onto a blank piece of paper snowy."

The lady mad grabbed Pen and tried to write her words few;
the paper showed no letters, lines, or art to view.
She too was caging all ideas within her mind.
When thoughts wanted out, freedom to them she declined.

She then picked up tired Pencil, moved it upside down,
and used its eraser to try to delete a frown
from her own sad face, since no visible ideas were
on the desktop or the paper, not even a blur.

The lady wasn't able to edit her face,
so Pen and Pencil were put back into their place
inside the pencil holder's gripping metallic wires
that blocked writing about problems, dreams, and desires.

Two computers blinked right above Pen and Pencil.
The lady's eyes shifted upward to pause until
she touched one computer's keyboard and was trying
to type some words, but not a word was appearing.

She chose to use the Internet to do some research;
she found some ideas, but her mind too much did search
for her own ideas or to paraphrase and quote.
Her edited ideas still were not free to float,
and her mind was overwhelmed with the large amount
of data she had read and could not even count.

For months, the lady tried some methods of prewriting:
freewriting, asking questions, listing, outlining,
and on pieces of paper, drawing diagrams
while using her pen, pencil, and computer programs.
The lady kept analyzing her prewriting,
thinking about purpose and audience while drafting
many papers with clear structures and strong details
that would logically lead readers down some great trails.

Drafting, revision, and editing then ensued,
until the lady's writing utensils had all viewed
her success at writing ideas on some blank paper,
rather than viewing an empty page's cold blur.

"I'll have to keep practicing my skillful new ways
of traversing within and around the writing maze
of prewriting, drafting, revising, and editing;
I'll then have more freedom for ideas to upswing."

Months later, the lady picked up Pen and Pencil
and wrote: "It's October 20th, when the thrill
of writing on the National Day on Writing
will be really possible, fun, and exciting."

"Now I can really write. I've been reading about

and thinking about my writing, while blanking out
my anxiety with practice and improved skills.
I now can write many words with creative thrills."

"I have the freedom to create many papers
because I now know when and how my writing occurs
while I prewrite, analyze, draft, revise, and edit
all of my creative ideas to readers transmit."

The lady wrote a new paper, which she then printed,
so she could write some comments on it as she read
it out loud. She then found and fixed some problems great
before progressing to many edits create.

Editing like many professional editors,
the lady did multiple enhancing explores
by reading her paper more than once while doing
some project, content, structure, and copy editing.

While employing her pen, pencil, and two computers,
she said to them all, "Thanks for your great work as tutors.
With my skills enhanced, I have more freedom of speech:
I can write to myself and to others outreach
with prewriting, drafting, revision, and editing,
while using many methods different to upswing."

The computer, Pen, and Pencil stood straight as they
prepared themselves to work a lot during a long day
of new writing and editing actions with less wrong
that would happen upon the hardness of a desk strong.

They knew the lady had enhanced her writing thrills
and would do better in life with all of her skills,
resulting in more pay raises, so she could now shop
for some blankets to soften the wooden desktop.

A Maze Poem: Costumes on Halloween

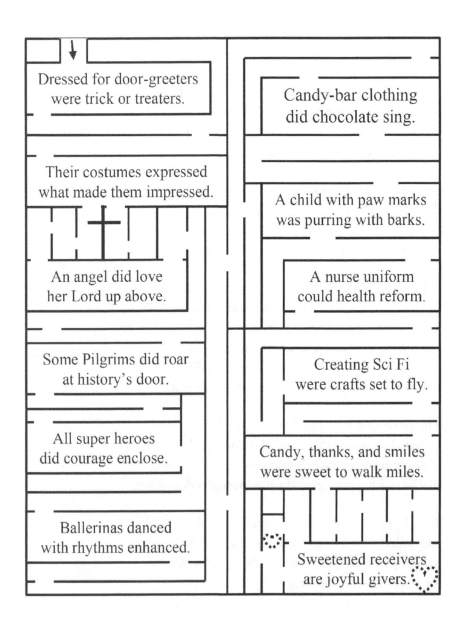

Dressed for door-greeters
were trick or treaters.

Candy-bar clothing
did chocolate sing.

Their costumes expressed
what made them impressed.

A child with paw marks
was purring with barks.

An angel did love
her Lord up above.

A nurse uniform
could health reform.

Some Pilgrims did roar
at history's door.

Creating Sci Fi
were crafts set to fly.

All super heroes
did courage enclose.

Candy, thanks, and smiles
were sweet to walk miles.

Ballerinas danced
with rhythms enhanced.

Sweetened receivers
are joyful givers.

Costumes on Halloween

Dressed for door-greeters
were trick or treaters.

Their costumes expressed
what made them impressed.

An angel did love
her Lord up above.

Some Pilgrims did roar
at history's door.

All super heroes
did courage enclose.

Ballerinas danced
with rhythms enhanced.

Candy-bar clothing
did chocolate sing.

A child with paw marks
was purring with barks.

A nurse uniform
could health reform.

Creating Sci Fi
were crafts set to fly.

Candy, thanks, and smiles
were sweet to walk miles.

Sweetened receivers
are joyful givers.

The Strength of Unity on Veterans Day

The wind of the day was flying against
a United States flag, fluttered and tensed,
but staying strong atop its tall steel pole
to fly against the wind's attempted control.

The wind and the flag paused their sky-fight flights
to watch a journey of flags at lower heights
in the hands of veterans who all were led
by red, white, and blue to move lives ahead.

While dressed for war and peace, veterans road-marched
with their rifles and flags moving upward arched
towards the hurling wind and the darkening clouds
overlooking the clapping hands of sidewalk crowds.

When the claps became louder, the wind returned
and hit the pole's flag, which made the flag concerned
about the small flags held by veterans proud
and their loved ones in the parade and the crowd.

The large flag waved at a group of musicians,
who played music while veterans clutched their guns,
focused on darkened clouds, and acted warlike
as they pulled triggers for a fictional strike.

No ammo real was used for parading joys,
but the cartridges blank did make enough noise
when paired with the music and hands clapping brave
to scare the wind and clouds to better behave.

The rays of the sun beamed through every star
of the tallest flag flying near and far
above the flags of clappers and veterans
to create rays of light for each star-shaped lens.

Flashing down, the star-shaped lights of many types
landed brightly atop the road's painted stripes,
connecting together with red, white, and blue,
so fifty states were in a single flag's view.

The flashing stars brightened the veterans' feet
as they marched forth strong atop the concrete street
while the flag high above their hats waved salutes
by moving in sync with the walking boots.

Members of the Army, Navy, Marine Corps,
Air Force, and Coast Guard all did so much more
in their service: they respectfully waved
at their country's people whom they had saved.

Freedom stayed strong on this Veterans Day
with marchers and watchers along the way
all waving to act as one, which relates
to the unity of the United States.

United States Flag

A May Flower in November 1620[6]

The flowers of May were blooming away
in summer's great warmth and fall's wintry air.
A petal broke off, went sailing astray,
into the wind, with a Separatist's prayer.

It paused in the sky with the blue turning gray;
then continued its trip 'til wooden beams were near.
When one of them cracked, the petal did say:
"I fear for my life! This storm's so unfair!"

"But I know, in this world, many are things unfixed."

"'cause I trust in my Lord, to Him I'll pray."
With prayers and repairs, the beam was soon fixed.
"I thank thee, Lord, for strengthening my 'May.'"
The voyage moved on; many problems eclipsed.
In November within a New World's bay,
the flower became Mayflower in-mixed.

Mayflower II, Plymouth, Massachusetts

Many Good Thanks in 2015[7]

Thanksgiving is a time when many people, including myself, are thankful to God for their many blessings. Just being alive and being able to say "thank you" to my Lord and to the many wonderful people in our world is a blessing all by itself.

T he
h eavenly
A lmighty's
n oisy
k indness
s trengthens
g rateful
I mpactful
v oices
I nto
n ew
g ratitudes

Many Good Thanks: A Prayer Poem[8]

To my Lord and Savior, Jesus Christ:

I praise you, Lord, for loving me
for many years in wondrous ways.
In sunny joy, my eyes can see
with all your guidance helping me.
I thank you, Lord, for being you.
Please bless yourself and others too.

Amen

Waiting in Advent

Crowded impatient feet are waiting at the sale
with toes fidgeting restlessly upon the trail
of Christmas shoppers crammed within a lengthy line
to purchase gifts in person, rather than online.

Near the end of the shopping line, four people stand
and talk about their Christmas gifts that have been planned.
One of the four people smiles and says, "We should stand
here longer before getting into that line, and
we should be sure we have all the gifts that we've planned
to buy." Other shoppers listen and understand
the four people are brethren who've been shopping and
finding presents that are now in each tired hand.

While staring strong at words beneath
a sign about an advent wreath,
one of the siblings points to the sign
and says, "That name of 'Hope' is mine,"
and I hope our presents will be
great enough for our parents' glee."

One of Hope's brothers points to the words
about Advent candles and says, "See,
'Love' is my favorite of those words,
so that's what my name always will be."

Next in the brethren's horizontal line
is another sister; she's wearing pink
and says, "If you want to know what I think,
then 'Joy' is the name that's joyfully mine."

Hope and Love both notice and love the joyful style
of Joy's hair as it curls and curls close to her smile.
All three of these family members then look down
at the fourth member's feet resting upon the ground.

The fourth member is wearing a purple shoe
on one foot. His other shoe's the color blue.
He stares at his shoes and says, "I'm wearing two
different shoes because, this morning, I knew
the season of Advent was starting anew.
In some churches, the purple candles are blue.
Right now, my name's 'Peace,' whether purple or blue."

Hope says, "The candle and lighting
differences aren't dividing
worshippers, who are all enticed
by the birthday of Jesus Christ."

Peace says, "You're absolutely right about that.
Religious freedom's a great welcoming mat.
Jesus enters many different homes at
times when worshippers are kneeling on each mat."

"Details in many groups at times
will differ. For instance, our rhymes
aren't exactly the same; each is
unique for each of us," Hope says.

"You're so right about differences.
In our scheduled shopping times and dates,
all of us had our preferences,
especially for today," Love states.

"Rhyming diversity can build a smile,"
Joy says, smiles, and adds, "I'm so thankful for
this shopping trip. We agreed to explore
this store and then to meet in this same aisle."

Love gives Joy a hug and says, "I know.
We have our similarities and
our differences. Even so, I glow
to attend events that we have planned."

Peace says, "I'm also so glad to be shopping,
but we should now be moving and not stopping.
here. We're near the end of a line and blocking
shoppers, who are turning and backwards walking."

Before the four begin to move, a stranger bumps
into the arm of Peace. Peace's coffee cup jumps
out of his hand, splashes onto his corduroy
jeans, and spills across the boots of Hope, Love, and Joy.

Hope says, "Peace, I hope you're okay."
That felt hot when it found its way
onto my boots, and my boots are
better shields than your clothes, by far."

Before Peace speaks, the stranger stares at the spilled coffee,
frowns, turns to walk away, and looks like he might flee.
He then stares at the Advent wreath, sighs, and says,
"Please forgive me. I messed up because shopping is
tough to do with these long lines. Last night, I began
to shop online, which for me is a better plan."

The stranger looks down and picks up the now-empty
coffee cup. He then gives the cup with a twenty-
dollar bill to Peace and says, "I'm really sorry
about ruining your day with your family."

"Thanks a lot," Peace says while putting the twenty
into his billfold. Then to the stranger, he
gives fifteen dollars and asks, "Do you really
think the four of us look like a family?

"Yeah, I do. I noticed Hope and Love were hugging
when I first came into the store. I was running
to do my shopping quickly. Five minutes later,
Joy's joyful from the hugs that were even greater
than the ones shared between Hope and Love. Finally,
Peace, you hugged a circle of hugs: your family."

The relatives step away from the lengthy line,
encircle one another to themselves align
into an advent circle next to the stranger
while softly talking and hugging one another.

The family circle then lights up nearby faces
by warmly shaking hands and smiling their embraces
to the arm-bumping stranger and other nearby
enlightened people who brightly smile in reply.

Love says, "Our smiles really show how close
together we all are and how we're
a family. The light of love glows
and brings some faraway people near."

The stranger tries to give back to Peace the fifteen
dollars, but Peace refuses to accept the green
cash and moves his red-sleeved elbow next to the green
cash, creating a peaceful Christmas-colored scene.

Peace says, "I'm fine. The coffee wasn't too hot,
and even replacing it won't cost a lot.
Taking more than five dollars from you will not
be fair." Peace looks at his jeans and adds, "I thought
last night about buying new jeans. These are not
that good anymore. Ten years ago, I bought
them. For years, they've been stained and now smell a lot
like coffee. While comfortable, handsome they're not."

The eyes of Peace turn to a shopper whose spot
is near the end of the line. The shopper's not
distraught about the line and no doubt forethought
a plan for the lengthy wait. She's eating hot
pizza. Peace smells the food and says, "I should not
be noticing other people's food, but ought
to enjoy and smell my own coffee for thought,
rather than smell other shoppers' food for thought."

The bumping stranger says, "You're loving your own view
of your own clothes. With old jeans, you're dressing like you
want to. Instead of loving other people's thoughts
about your jeans, you'd rather just love your own thoughts."

The Advent shoppers all smile. Then an employee
enters their circle of happiness, hastily
mops the spilled coffee away from the floor, and says,
"Since spilled coffee is no longer on this spot, the longest line of all is
now the shortest."

The bumping stranger steps close to the employee
and says, "That's backwards. Coffee helps people to be
faster, which means less time and less space are wasted
when real unspilled coffee is present and tasted."

The employee says, "Whether shorter or longer,
when joined together, time and space are both stronger.
Smelling coffee anywhere makes me stronger feel:
I grip a coffee mug's handle with hands of steal."

The bumping stranger bumps into the employee
and says, "I'm sorry for moving so quickly. We
should be getting into line right now while it's not
super-long. Which one of us should take the first spot?"

Peace looks at the arm-bumping stranger, surveys
the twenty people in line, and says, "Delays

for four are longer than for one. A sideways
step to that line for you, not for us, conveys
our kindness. While moving to the not-always-
cash register, we hope you find many ways
to keep yourself busy and not in a daze."

The bumping stranger says, "Thanks a lot. You're all so
hopeful, loving, joyful, and peaceful." Steps are slow
as the stranger, Hope, Love, Joy, and Peace all enter
the line and curve it slightly. They clearly prefer
to remain in a circle of family shoppers,
rather than in a line of credit-card payers.

The line has some sad shoppers with nothing to do;
they seem really anxious and are complaining, too,
to each other about the too-long double line,
their need for more time, and an upcoming deadline.
Joy smiles at the shoppers and says, "Some time is ours.
Even if a day's length grows by ten hours,
we'll still want three hundred and three more hours,
and the power to make thousands more hours
by growing more hours like we grow flowers.
Our time is a measure of life that empowers."

The sad shopper who is carrying a new clock
to buy slowly moves her mouth to a curvy mock
of a half-smile and then smiles a real smile at Joy.
"You're right about time. In my garden, to enjoy
the growth of time, more plants may or may not appear
to grow quickly, depending on the time of year."

Hope says, "I always hope my plants
will grow so fast they'll avoid ants
and other problems. Waiting can
be tough, unless we have a plan
of action to keep us busy

with merry acts to do and see."
Two once-sad shoppers take out their cell phones and do
the same actions as a few waiting-in-line new
shoppers are doing. Some seem glad-to-be-busy
shoppers. One smiling face is part of a selfie.

Looking at cell phones are other merry people;
who see Facebook, emails, and ad prices; and pull
up information about the best store to go
to or a website with shipments not very slow.

One happy shopper orders twenty gifts online
while waiting to pay for a computer in line.

On people's cell phones, text messages are exchanged;
gift ideas are discussed, and Christmas plans arranged.

After watching some sad shoppers
become happy busy shoppers,
Hope asks her relatives, "Should we
buy that advent wreath? It could be
a great early Christmas present
for our parents, who love advent
and would so love another wreath
to circle candles like a sheath."

Love looks quickly at the wreath and its candles.
He says, "That's a great idea! I'm glad
we were named after Advent candles.
We should buy that wreath for Mom and Dad,
so they can have a lot of candles
and another wreath to make them glad."

Joy says, "Today's the first day of Advent
when the first purple candle should be lit.
I'll leave this line, get the wreath, and buy it.
We'll then have an early Christmas present."

Peace says, "It's so wonderful how we're waiting
while also doing hopeful, joyful, loving,
and peaceful collaboration of buying
a wreath and candles for illuminating
our lives to be ready for the upcoming
celebration of the birthday and praising
of Jesus, who is many lives brightening.
Right now, we should definitely be stepping
out of line and buying what we've been thinking
of buying for a part of today's shopping."

The first of the Advent shoppers to step out of
the lengthy line is Hope; she's followed by Love,
Joy, and Peace. All four move backwards toward the Advent
wreath and candles. Hope picks up the wreath, and its scent
makes her and other shoppers smile. Hope then pauses
to stare at the sets of candles; her pause causes
Love to help pick out the candles being studied
the most by Hope, Joy, and Peace. Love displays her speed
with a quick choice. Her relatives all understand
a need for agreement about what's being planned,
so they all shake their heads, showing their support of
the wreath and candle choices made by Hope and Love.

The smiling Advent family moves to the back
of the line. After a few seconds, a small crack
in the middle of the line keeps growing until
there's enough empty space for four people to fill
in the line's open space. The newly empty spot
is right behind the bumping stranger's current slot.

The bumping stranger and the Christmas shoppers all
wave hands at the Advent family to not stall,
but to rather jump into their initial spot
in the long line of shoppers. Joy says, "Thanks a lot,"
as she and her joyful family members walk

back into their original spot. They then talk
to one another about their plans for shopping
up until Christmas when shopping will be stopping.

The bumping stranger, while positioned directly
in front of Hope, says, "You must love your family
a lot to plan on meeting each other for fun
in this department's line even though everyone
in your family is holding onto presents
that were carried here from different departments."

Hope says, "I love my family
and really love the chance to be
together while spending some time
shopping and waiting in line. I'm
even very thankful the line
we're waiting in is a long line."

The bumping stranger says, "You're so right; family
time spent waiting together can be so happy.
I'm thinking about gifts my parents might prefer.
Can people today buy gold, frankincense, and myrrh
as Christmas gifts? For my parents, I want to buy
and give to them some nice presents, like the Magi
did for Jesus when the Wise Men—all three—
visited Jesus Christ, the one who will be
our Lord and Savior for all eternity."

"Gifts of gold, frankincense, and myrrh
are great," Hope says to the stranger.
"I'll have to buy them at some time."
Hope moves her hands up and adds, "I'm
already going to buy these
two matching watches, which will please
my parents. They really love when
they exercise together. Then

they both can total and compare
their counted calories, which they share
with each other and their friends, too.
With these new watches, my two
parents will let the watches count
and add their calorie amount
for them as they're exercising
together and wearing matching
fitness watches that lovingly
were given to them both by me."
The watches in Hope's hand attract the stranger's eyes.
He says, "Those look like awesome gifts, but exercise
isn't done too much by my too-busy parents.
They both love Christmas decorations and events,
so I'll be buying them gifts with Christmas themes, and
gold, frankincense, and myrrh'll remind them of the land
where Jesus was born, Bethlehem, and where the Magi
brought their gifts, contained in treasure chests. These Magi
were very wise men. They came to worship Jesus,
who took our sins away and gifted love to us."

Love says, "I'm sure your parents will love
such a wonderful present from you.
I'll be showing my parents my love
by using these frames as points of view
for some new pictures to hang above
a fireplace's flaming debut
in a family room we all love
with its warming hearts for photos new."

The bumping stranger says, "I love those picture frames
so much. Just thinking of the warmth of heated flames
underneath some picture frames is a pretty clear
view into a family's warming atmosphere."

Joy raises her hands and shows everyone
her chosen gift cards that she'll be giving
to friends and family who like waiting
'til after Christmas for some shopping fun.

Peace smiles at Joy's gift cards and raises his hands
high enough for everyone to see. His hands
are holding cell phones. "Everyone understands
the importance of communication plans
to go with these phones. I'm holding in my hands
what I'll be buying: both the phones and the plans."

The bumping stranger says, "Gifts for talking are great
because people can easily communicate
with one another, whether they're separated
from each other or very closely connected
to one another, like Advent relatives and
nearby strangers with no missing coffee in hand."

Peace says, "Shortly, I can buy some more coffee.
Thanks to your money, I can buy it for free."

The stranger says, "Since I spilled all your coffee, Peace,
you and your brethren's time in this line should decrease.
We should switch places, so you and your family
can all just step forward and be in front of me."

Peace says, "Thanks, but we did choose to leave the line,
so staying right here is really very fine."

The stranger says, "There's another reason for me
to have you step forward and be in front of me.
I'm buying gifts chosen by Wise Men; each present
was given to Jesus after his birth. Advent,
though, is an earlier season about waiting
for Jesus's birth. The Advent wreath you're buying
signifies a time before the Wise Men's visit,

so you should step forward and in front of me fit."
The stranger walks backward and softly shakes the hands
of all until behind the family he stands.

The Advent family thanks the now-touching and
not-bumping man for his kindness and helping hand.
The family then begins to discuss the price
of the candles and the wreath; they seem as precise
as cashiers, dividing the cost into amounts
of four. While Joy's and Peace's credit-card accounts
will be used, Hope and Love will happily give cash
to help Joy and Peace with the gift's cost in a flash.

While moving within the line so slow,
Love says, "I do love waiting in line
when family and friends are also
waiting with me for the divine,
upcoming event that will occur
when we worship Christ on His birthday:
we'll light the candle in the center
of the Advent wreath on Christmas Day."

Peace steps sideways, moves forward to slowly go
super close to the touching-stranger's elbow,
and says, "You're so right, Love. We also have so
many great friends today. Our new friend's aglow
when people bump into him, hug him, and slow
their busy lives to help him and cause no woe."
Peace softly bumps the stranger, his love to show.

The stranger says, "Hope, Love, Joy, and Peace do flow, grow,
glow, and bestow themselves onto others. I'm so
happy to have met you all in this lengthy line,
where we've had the time to talk online and off-line."

Hope laughs and asks, "Are we on-line
or in-line?" She looks at a sign

advertising the store's website
and says, "Both answers can be right,
especially if we're buying
on our phones while in-line standing."

Before long, the Advent family has enjoyed
the lengthy time waiting in line and has arrived
at the line's beginning. They each pay for their own
presents first, before the group gift. Working alone
for this line's a cashier with a nametag: "Christian."
Two Advent family members contribute ten
dollars each to pay half of the forty dollars
due for both the candles and the wreath. Two dollars
and eighty cents more than what had been planned is due
because Christian adds taxes to the total, too.

Peace smiles and says, "I'll pay the extra money
because of the extra cash given to me
by our newest friend." Peace bumps the stranger's knee
and adds, "Thanks so much for helping me to be
the taxpayer today for my family.
Our gift of the Advent wreath will be tax-free."

Love says, "Thanks to you, Peace. You're always
so helpful. I've also been thinking
of the birth of Jesus, which relays
so many reasons for worshipping
God and His Son, as well as to praise
the Holy Spirit. They're so loving."

Hope says, "Talking about Advent
while we're paying for an Advent
wreath is great. I especially
like to think about what will be
a future event with our Lord
Jesus Christ that's often ignored

by people: His second coming.
Advent's not just signifying
His birth; it's also proclaiming
a future day of His coming
for all the Christians He's saving."

Christian smiles and gives a big bag containing
the wreath and candles to Peace, who is now holding
two bags. Christian then says, "You all have great presents
and know about the loving eternal presence
of God, who's with us at this busy shopping mall
and every other place. The greatest gift of all
is the salvation we've been given through God's son,
Jesus Christ, who's within all lines, the number one."

The Advent family members all step backward,
and Peace moves the bag containing the wreath forward.
The wreath is now the first in line. After a few
short seconds of waiting, the wreath's bag is moved to
the center of the Advent family's newly-
formed circle. Eight hands clasp together; shoppers see
the family's hands are still gripping their purses and
shopping bags while clasped to each other. Every hand
is holding another hand with a bag between
the hands and sometimes two bags with a purse between.

The Advent family's circle of love attracts
the touching stranger, who's paid for his gifts and acts
as if he wants to join the circle, which opens
for him. Everyone trades info with Christmas pens.

"On Facebook, we now can become each other's friends,"
the stranger says within his circle of new friends.
The family and new friend take turns bumping
and hugging each other as the circle's turning.

The cell phone of Hope loudly rings.

She answers, says "yes," and then flings
both her purse and her bags up to
her shoulder. "I should drive to
the house of my best friend. She needs
a ride when it snows since she speeds
too much and worries about loss
of time. I can help her to cross
over the loss of time in life
and guide her to drive with less strife."

Peace says, "I'm glad your friend has you to help her.
Will you join us at our parents' house after?"

Hope says, "Yes, I'll soon see you all
when we talk about this crammed mall
with our parents while we're eating
dinner, praising God, and lighting
the first candle in the brand new
wreath placed in a high point of view."

The Advent family and new-found friend exchange
some gifts of touches, bumps, and hugs. They re-arrange
their bags and purses while leaving the shopping mall.
When the friends are outside, they form a circle small
within the parking lot. A beam of the sun's light
lands in the center of the circle of smiles bright.

The Advent family circles the ray of light,
enjoying the warming presence of the white light,
which signifies the purity of Christ's birthday;
this candle's lit on Christmas Eve or Christmas day.

While leaving, Hope waves happily
at her new friend and family;
they wave at her waves while thinking
of their Advent meal upcoming.

After Hope leaves the circle, four others remain
to spend some more time waiting with loved ones to gain
the warmth of fellowship with family and friends
while planning their presents and holiday weekends.

An angry stranger walks up to the circle and asks,
"Why do you all need to stand here and do your own tasks
so far into this small lane in this lot for parking
that you're blocking too many people who are trying
to quickly leave and then wait in even longer lines?
When you block traffic, you should pay lots of traffic fines."

The friended stranger says, "You're so right. We're standing
here, should move elsewhere, and are way too much talking.
We've been thanking our Lord for the great miraculous
gift of eternal salvation, advantageous
in adding time for those wise-shopping someones
who are waiting in line to buy gifts for loved ones
or not waiting while buying gifts online and then
still waiting for a delivery to happen.
Advent's a time of waiting for Jesus to come
again, so Christians can all have a great outcome."

While listening to the hopefulness, joy, and love
of Peace's words, the new stranger becomes one of
the circle of family and friends, who all smile
at each other while stepping back into a pile
of snow between two parked cars. They're now not blocking
the traffic, and instead, like candles, are melting
the pile of snow and lighting up the parking lot
while exchanging joyful smiles with shoppers a lot.

The new stranger sees new lines of shoppers; each line is
forming with its shoppers turned to face his line; he says,
"Your family's now indirectly blocking traffic,
but I do think this indirect traffic's terrific

because the people are hearing each other and us;
they then want to stand in this encircling line with us,
so they can enjoy spending some of their time waiting
with and connecting to the Advent joys upcoming."

Joy says, "I so love the miraculous
gift of salvation: Jesus. The Christians
who worship His birth through the waiting lens
of Advent see time as advantageous."

Love says, "You're right. We all have the time
to love our wait in line with neighbors
who touch, bump, and hug at anytime
they want to connect to some shoppers,
but sometimes, we need to be leaving.
We need to bring our wreath of Advent
to our parents' house tonight. Lighting
the new wreath will be a bright event."

The touchers, bumpers, and huggers within the lines
wave to one another with their hearts, souls, and minds
visible to shoppers with eyes that love to see
the candled lights of Love, her friends, and family,
who are all connecting, like wise men and women,
when they end their shopping spree by saying "Amen."

A Forevergreen Christmas

A
star atop
a
tree
had light
so bright its
evergreen ornaments
foresaw it as the baby Sun
created by God to perpetuate roots
and draw other lights to the decorated tree.
Outdoors at night,
shadows were hidden
and green branches forbidden
from growing into places without light.
From heaven, the baby Son saw the shadows
and prepared His light for the branches to enclose
the evergreen's trunk with their forever-green delight.
The branches twinkled with joy about the soon-to-be-born
new Sun who'd adorn
their tree to be forevergreen.
Amid the advent of tree-hugging
lights and green-needle crowns for a king,
a branch-kissing angel of an ornament appeared
to shepherd ornaments, who went quickly and neared
the Joseph and Mary ornaments, who were praying within
the manger scene; they were thankful for the Son on the earth.
Forevergreen branches spread their brightness to celebrate the birth
of their
Lord &
Savior
Jesus
Christ.

The Growth of Time on a Happy Birthday

The cake was just created and more did grow
with each passing moment of a timely show
as mom and dad added candy to delight
atop the strawberry cake with frosting white.

A candy garden, growing on the frosting,
had birds with open mouths ready to sing
and butterflies with extended wings to fly
amid circling flowers with a tree high.

A butterfly fell from the top of the tree,
landed on a piece of red-flower candy,
shifted its wings to twist its mouth to bite
the center of the candy's sweet delight.

The sweetened mouth of the butterfly did grow
with added size and colors like a rainbow
while its body did intake the new food
to become as large as the birds being viewed.

The wings of candied birds did flap with joy
to have a butterfly grow up and enjoy
becoming a part of a birthday scene
that soon would sprout within a time machine.

Candles planted in the garden of frosting
were lit to shine their warmth on those who did sing
"Happy Birthday" to the person who had grown
an added year to thrive in a new time zone.

Past pictures were shown and memories were shared
while new pictures were taken and compared
to make some more memories that would travel
forward for future years of growth to retell.

The Joys of Learning on Graduation Day

Commencement was already beginning
when some ready students began helping
a few late students who were not yet ready
in their caps and gowns to become ready.

The timely students showed the ones who were late
positions for their caps and gowns to be straight;
both groups discussed the process of forming lines
and helped each other with many guidelines.

Before long, the students with music were joined
as they walked forward with new groups conjoined;
all were now ready for the day's commencement
of enhanced lives during and after this event.

While people were standing, smiling, and watching,
the students in caps and gowns were moving
in lines in front of cell phones, flashing for all
on their way to the front of the greatest hall.

After hearing the national anthem, people
heard a speech about using their skills to pull
past dreams into the future, so commencement
could move forward with them via their present.

When other speeches did finish their sounds,
the clapping hands made their own clapping sounds,
and cheerful yells added aural emotions
as hands went upward in joyful motions.

The college president introduced Spree,
the student speaker, who stepped forth with glee
to start her motivating oration
about her own learning and education.

Spree's hand was shaking with anxiety
as she touched the mike while trying to be
less nervous about her speech being taped
and heard in a giant room that was star-shaped.

While slowly inhaling and exhaling,
Spree looked at the students who were judging
as they stared back at her. Some of the faces
she knew. Others weren't even acquaintances.

Spree thought of her speech classes and then could see
methods of calming her nervous anxiety.
She began to smile; her now-joyful face
connected to her audience's embrace.

Spree said, "While today, I'm getting my degree,
I'm still learning more and am truly happy.
Learning is a logical control key;
it unlocks and enhances our identity."

The heads of the people in the audience
moved up and down, showing agreement intense
with Spree's view of the importance of learning
more each day, so mental growth will upswing.

Presenting her speech with lots of smiles, Spree
showed her love for learning, and all could see
her feelings upon her face. Her moving hands
emphasized her love for her future plans.

Spree said, "I hope all of your learning journeys
will be strong, like mine have been, so fears will ease.

My learning here today has set me free
to give speeches with lessened anxiety."

After this inspiring ending to Spree's speech,
everyone's clapping hands to her did reach
to strongly support her by being happy
to clap her speech as great to hear and to see.

After the next person's speech, some students stood,
walked to the stage's stairs that looked so good,
and switched into an alphabetical line,
which slowly moved onto the stairs' incline.

The student first in line, Al, did not know
what time across the wooden stage to go;
the college's president waved her hand,
showing him when and where to walk and to stand.

Al sauntered slowly toward the stage's center,
nervously smiled at the photographer,
received his degree, shook hands with people,
and looked around at friends in the room so full.

A hand in the crowd kept moving like a guide
from the right side of her head to the left side.
Al said, "Whoops," slid to the left his cap's tassel,
smiled at cameras, and felt no more hassle.

The other students had carefully watched Al
as he had crossed the stage, so now they all
thought they had learned all they needed to know
to cross the stage for their diplomas aglow.

The president looked mad and waved at Ann
to walk into the center of the stage. Ann ran
because she was quite good at analysis
and had quickly realized she was amiss.

People knew Ann had taken too long to move
to a position the president would approve
because the president had combined a frown
with her angered hand that had waved around.

Ann learned she should have studied better to gauge
the timing before Al had walked off the stage.
The president then smiled at Ann, who smiled, too,
since her error was small, as they both now knew.

When Ann received and held her diploma, she
analyzed her degree and instantly could see
she was ready for her career. Her face filled
with joy: she was now more qualified and skilled.

Ann's error helped her and others with learning
to think about on-stage spacing and timing
analytically. Ann was instantly free
to leave the stage with hands clapping happily.

The next student to cross the stage was Art.
A painting of an easel was a major part
of her cap's square top. To add to the painting,
a real brush atop the easel's image did cling.

When Art was handed her diploma, she stared
at it for a few seconds before she shared
her happy thoughts and smart feelings about the kind
of art contained inside its structure and design.

"I love this design. I never before knew
about the beauty of an emotional view
of forms. This diploma feels so very fine
within its lovely paper and font design."
Art lovingly stroked her diploma, hugged it,
shook hands with the people on stage, stepped a bit
forward, bowed to everyone, and happily

went back to her seat, where she kissed her degree.

Com had seen and heard the past interactions.
Previous students with various actions
had walked across the stage so helpfully;
he now knew how to cross the stage correctly.

In order to continue with his progress
while he communicated his thankfulness
for his skills in a clear and courteous way,
Com headed onto the stage with no delay.

The president thanked Com for volunteering
in so many ways, including his writing
of campus newspaper articles printed
on paper and campus-wide distributed.

With a smile, Com communicated his joy
about his enhanced skills that he'd employ
to work for him within his new career
of reading, writing, and speaking far and near.

As Com stepped toward the stage's left side stairs,
he paused to stare at some of his puzzled peers
who were looking on their phones for his writings;
he realized he should start some online things.

Econ, with an economics interest,
next walked on stage with bills on her cap pressed.
Numbers and words were written atop the bills,
showing her financial literacy skills.

Just like the stock market and interest rates,
Econ would sometimes fall down; her classmates
would always help her to rise back up again,
and now, while climbing the stairs, she fell again.

Econ landed on the stage's right side
in front of Nurs, who soon would be certified
with helpful skills through her nursing degree
and knowledge of acting professionally.

Nurs helped Econ to stand while saying quickly,
"We'll pick up those fallen bills, and I'm really
very sorry for not standing close to you;
I then could have stopped your fall by catching you."

The bills were placed on cap with classmates' support.
Econ said, "Thank you all so much. Your import
and export activities are really nice!
For many fields, you have skills and advice."

"You're so welcome, Econ. Being ready
with skills from multiple fields is the key
to success for every activity
and can help us to learn and to healthy be."

Econ climbed the stairs, crossed the stage with fast feet,
received her diploma, and walked to her seat,
where she studied her surroundings carefully
to ensure they were structured successfully.

Ed was next to climb the stairs and cross the stage;
the tiny pictures on top his cap did engage
people who felt education's importance
to enable and help their lives to commence.

While Ed was shaking the president's hand,
the video display of his cap was grand
on the giant screen, and visible to all
were some icons of standards and outcomes tall.

The edge of Ed's cap had common-core details
displayed with photos of students, males and females,

actively building skills while learning content
by pursuing their goals and outcomes augment.

The center of Ed's cap showed some learning techniques:
listening, note-taking, creating critiques,
drawing while reading out loud, writing, speaking,
and boosting skills while content memorizing.

Matt was next with a small screen on his cap's top.
Changing icons made the screen look like a laptop
that was displaying numbers and words in code.
Matt's wisdom about math and computers showed.

While Matt climbed up the stairs, his eyes bounced between
the wooden stage's left and right sides to glean
geometric data that his mind could use
to determine useful numbers to peruse.

After Matt received his degree, he returned
to his seat and texted a friend: "I've learned
another skillful method for me to build
a brand new porch! My parents will be so thrilled!"

Matt's parents were at his graduation
and watched him closely until he was done
texting his friend. Matt's mom then texted to Matt:
"We love to see how you always can chat."

Matt then realized his parents were watching;
he blushed because he knew about not texting
sometimes. He then texted: "Automatically,
I keep doing this. Thanks for reminding me."

Matt's mom texted back: "I also am texting,
so both of us are wrong for disrespecting
the people on the stage. My phone's going off."
Matt texted back: "Mine's also going off."

Matt and his mom both put their phones away;
Matt was hoping other texters would delay
their cell-phone usage for a more correct time
if they saw 'twas wrong to text at such a time.

Many people in the room were texting still,
but Sience, one of Matt's friends, saw that Matt's skill
was not to text right now, but to act correctly,
to teach others to also act correctly.

After Matt and Sience had each turned off a phone,
other students noticed and turned off their own;
cell-phone usage was now completely stopping,
like a sci-fi event was really happening.

Thea, the next student seen climbing the stairs,
made the focus of the audience's stares
be upon her noisy four-inch leather heels
that were clapping with each stare of joyful feels.

Thea's heels seemed to be gladly posturing
as Thea had taught them to do while acting
on real theatrical stages and stairways
for years of supporting her actions in plays.

Upon the stage, Thea's heels started clicking;
they wanted their positions to keep changing,
so they could both show themselves to the people
studying trips across the stage: their steep hill.

Thea's left shoe was precise and moved slowly;
then her right shoe moved forward, cutting quickly
in front of her left shoe and turning to show
people the word of "May" painted on its toe.

The numbers on the front of Thea's left shoe
conveyed the rest of the day's date, so people knew

the left shoe should be staying on the left side
and the right shoe should stay on the right side.

Sounding like words were noises from scraping shoes:
"My month's always first, so we'll not confuse
the audience about positions and passwords."
"But numbers are far more important than words."

"No, they aren't! Words are most important of all.
My word's read first, so even with our heels both tall,
my one word does many more important things than
your multiple too-slow numbers ever can."

The left shoe angrily kicked the right shoe's heel;
it wanted to step into its space ideal,
instead of being forced to move sideways
and switch its pre-planned straight path into a maze.

The right shoe moved back and kicked the left shoe's toe,
scraping the rose that was painted to show
Thea's love for this graduation date
and her desire to stage a setting great.

With kicks to claim some extra time and space,
Thea's shoes moved Thea to her perfect place
with no serious injuries to her feet
and just minor shoe scrapes, which almost looked sweet.

"I love your highest of interactive heels,
and the thorn scraped into the rose reveals
the reality of mazes very widespread
within every journey," the president said.

Thea glanced down at her now well-behaved shoes.
"Their stage rage is showing their differing views
about diverse educated journeys
across a stage with an audience to please."

Thea added, "While stage rage is often a fight
between actors and an audience impolite,
my heels did just betwixt themselves nicely prance,
so they could love and be loved by their audience."

The president smiled when Thea's heels were sweet
as they politely left the stage and then did greet
other graduated shoes who could interlace
in front of seats in the audience's space.

Theo was next to climb the stairs; his hands did pray,
thanking God for such a miraculous day.
His sister was here because she'd been healed
and was watching him walk toward his chosen field.

The president's smile showed admiration
for Theo's generous participation
in the college's bible-club activities,
and his student-government expertise.

Theo saw the president's extended hand
and moved his own to connect to hers, as planned.
He moved a golden cross from his hand into
the president's hand and said, "This is for you."

The president looked at the cross and said, "You
have always been so very helpful and true
to everyone. Thanks so much, and I hope you
will have as great of a life as is possible."

"Thank you! I've been learning so much by reading,
writing, listening, taking notes, studying,
and doing many other activities,
so I can move forward in my life with ease."

Theo's smile became linked to his happy eyes,
emitting tears of joy being sent to baptize

the smile of a major in theology
as he continued on his Christian journey.

When Theo left the stage, he moved his left hand
onto the wooden cross on his necklace and
then touched his ear as all in the audience
saw the bible verse on his cap grow intense.

A person doing some videotaping
was curious about the verse and was zooming
in to read it. A verbal image was made,
and the bible verse was on the screen displayed.

Some could easily see, read, and hear the verse
while others read it out loud to hear the verse:
"An intelligent mind acquires knowledge,
and the ear of the wise seeks knowledge" (Prov. 18:15: NRSV).

Crossing the stage next were hundreds of students
who were learning more and more about events
connected to graduation ceremonies,
advanced skills, new careers, and more degrees.

When standing off stage, students clapped their respect
to friends and the speakers who were so adept.
When seated, students sometimes spoke of insights
about upcoming grad event invites.

Seated next to each other were Lit and Writ,
who were happily talking with just a bit
of noise by texting themselves on their cell phones
and then sharing messages by switching phones.

"Lit, I loved taking that writing course with you."
"I loved it so much, too, Writ, and learned to do
so much better revision and editing
through our comments, quizzes, reading, and listening."

After moving phones back and forth with no upgrade,
Writ and Lit decided their numbers to trade,
so they now could text each other directly
and be friends for future contact frequently.

Both Writ and Lit changed their process of texting
each other, which resulted in revising
their communication to better transfer
their words, rather than their phones, with each other.

Lit and Writ then edited their process
by giving themselves easier access
to each other's words; they became repairers:
adding punctuation and fixing their errors.

Writ texted: "Since we've both revised our process,
we're doing more editing to better express
ourselves when sending items to each other's phones
than when we were just writing on our own phones."

In the row behind Writ and Lit were many
graduating students with diplomas plenty.
Some of the happy hands were silently texting;
others were clapping while mouths were softly talking.

Rea, who loved to read and was hoping
to work in a library, started talking
to the person next to her, whose preferred list
of future jobs began with sociologist.

"Socie, I'm so glad to now have my degree
resting in my hand while I'm getting ready
for my first professional job interview.
I'm hoping to get a librarian job new."

Socie smiled while waving her own diploma
and said, "I'm looking for a job, too, Rea.

I think my parents bought me a big present,
which might be a car, so I can drive content."

Rea looked at her phone while shaking her head.
"Here's an interesting article to read
on a website with charts and statistics
of the U.S. Bureau of Labor Statistics."

Rea smiled while adding, "This article says
'earnings increase and unemployment decreases
as educational attainment rises.'[9]
More money and jobs will be our best prizes."

Socie said, "You're so right, but even money
is not as important as the chance to be
myself: to do what my personality
really wants: to make my inner self happy."

Rea touched the top of her cap quickly,
where her love for books was literally
displayed with a photo taken lovingly
at the Rhode Island State House's library.

As Rea's fingers caressed her cap's photo,
her hand touched hands with the library clock's glow,
making the clock's hands appear to turn slowly
back in time, bouncing to a cap of history.

On Histore's cap stood a statue enthrall
of Roger Williams, who wanted freedom for all
when he founded Rhode Island with Christian grace;
liberty of the soul did he embrace.

The statue clasped a book like a book-lover
with "soul" and "liberty" on the book's cover.
Histore's head shifted up; his statue's eyes
moved skyward, too, just like Histore: wise.

The time arrived for grads to toss their caps
into the air. One cap was sporty, perhaps,
since it flew like a basketball from one place
into a distant parking lot's empty space.

Sporty's cap hit a car, jumped into a road,
and finally paused for Sporty as it slowed
itself and traffic; the cars all stopped, like fans,
to watch Sporty spot his cap near two sedans.

Competition then began: the cars were first
in moving forward; second, Sporty traversed
the road and parking lot with his cap in hand
until he was back in graduation's heartland.

Sporty's fans did clap their hands when they were shown
the basketball and hoop upon his cap sewn.
The ball's learned toss was landing in the hoop
as love for all winning graduates in the group.

One fan was Mu, whose phone's music played forth
in time to her own cap flying south to north,
which was high up on the scale of caps flying
and rhythmically moving, so students were singing.

Over the group next flew Pollit's cap in the air;
people were blind to see logos on his cap's square.
Was he a Democrat, a Republican,
or possibly a truly independent man?

No one knew the truth about Pollit until
he stepped closer to people and showed true skill
at helping them know the importance of voting
to support himself, rightful views, and good leaders.

Scientific caps went flying high and low
while flipping around in windy air to show

their pictures of astronomy, chemistry,
physics, geology, and biology.

Many other caps were enjoying the air
and flying sky high to participate and share
their knowledge and desires for future learning
to fulfill their dreams and even more upward spring.

After the cap tossing, phones began flashing
so much that many eyes were upward blinking
to stay open for pictures soon to appear
on Facebook for families and friends to cheer.

The upward blinks of educated eyes
showed the brightness of education's rise
while applying diverse past learning journeys
into future stage crossings of brilliant ease.

Library in the Rhode Island State House, Providence, Rhode Island

Roger Williams Statue in Roger Williams
Park, Providence, Rhode Island

A Prayer Poem at a Wedding

Our thanks to our Lord and Savior,
for every wedding's a loving door
that's opened for those who adore
the wonders of a shared rapport
within a home with ceilings lit
by heaven's lights, mazing through sunlit
windows, and landing on moonlit
yards and floors, structured to commit
to heavy feet being lightened
with glowing love for God transcend.
Thanks for love, again and again.
In Jesus' name we pray,
Amen

Endnotes

1   "holiday, n.", *OED Online,* Oxford University Press (March 2018). http://www.oed.com/view/Entry/87719?rskey=Xs2i6N&result=1 (accessed May 31, 2018).

2   Robert Frost, "The Road Not Taken," *Mountain Interval* (New York: Henry Holt and Company, 1921), 9.

3   Ibid.

4   William Bradford, (1651), quoted on National Monument to the Forefathers NRHP reference # 74002033 (Plymouth, Massachusetts, 1889).

5   Karen Petit, "Freedom to Worship God," rogerwill.com, (January 29, 2016). http://www.rogerwill.com/freedom-blog. (accessed December 16, 2017).

6   Karen Petit, "Many Good Thanks," *mayflowerdreams.com,* (August 29, 2014). http://www.mayflowerdreams.com/blog. (accessed December 16, 2017).

7   Karen Petit, "Many Good Thanks," *mayflowerdreams.com,* (November 3, 2015). http://www.mayflowerdreams.com/blog. (accessed June 30, 2018).

8   Karen Petit, "Many Good Thanks," *mayflowerdreams.com,* (December 1, 2015). http://www.mayflowerdreams.com/blog. (accessed June 30, 2018).

9   Dennis Vilorio, "Education matters," *Career Outlook,* U.S. Bureau of Labor Statistics (March 2016). https://www.bls.gov/careeroutlook/2016/data-on-display/education-matters.htm (accessed March 3, 2018).

About the Author

Dr. Karen Petit (www.drkarenpetit.com) is the author of five Christian books: *Banking on Dreams, Mayflower Dreams, Roger Williams in an Elevator, Unhidden Pilgrims,* and *Holidays Amaze.* Petit received her bachelor's, master's, and doctorate degrees in English from the University of Rhode Island. She loves to write, in addition to helping others to write.

Banking on Dreams is a Christian suspense/romance novel about a bank teller who likes ballroom dancing; she uses lucid dreaming techniques to help herself overcome nightmares about a bank vault. The Rhode Island setting, a robbery, and historic elements all add interesting components to this novel.

Mayflower Dreams has a protagonist who embarks on a real journey and a "dream story" as she explores the history and culture of the Pilgrims. She finds her modern life has connections to the Pilgrims. While fictional, this novel has historically accurate parts, such as quotes from historic figures, the "Mayflower Compact," 107 endnotes, 20 bible quotes, and a Pilgrim Language section. Photos from Plymouth tourist attractions are included in this novel.

Roger Williams in an Elevator, a Christian suspense novel, has a protagonist who becomes trapped in a partially destroyed building and helps people inside of eight different elevators: yelling, accounting, liberty, watery, fiery, falling, sharing, and hidden. The different elevator communities create their own rules and freedoms. The impact of Roger Williams on our society is seen in this novel's plot, characters, dream/reality connections, symbols, 69 endnotes, 14 bible quotes, and photos of statues, historic items, and the Rhode Island State House.

Unhidden Pilgrims is a Christian novel that connects free speech to religious freedom, dreams to reality, and the present to the past with action-filled scenes and pictures of historic items in Providence, Rhode Island, and Plymouth, Massachusetts. The protagonist sometimes has to run, hide, and fight; at other times, she stands her ground, becomes visible, and shares her faith and her love.

Holidays Amaze is Petit's most recent book, in addition to being her first published book of poetry. This author has been writing poetry for decades, including poetry for her master's degree in English with a Creative Writing focus. *Holidays Amaze* has content about holidays, as well as a wide variety of poetic structures, such as maze poems, prayer poems, traditional sonnets, and narratives.

Dr. Karen Petit has an author website (www.drkarenpetit.com) with links to her book websites, each of which has a blog:

- a dream blog at www.bankingondreams.com
- a "Many Good Thanks" blog at www.mayflowerdreams.com
- a freedom blog at www.rogerwill.com
- a sharing faith blog at www.unhiddenpilgrims.com
- a holiday blog at www.holidaysamaze.com

Petit loves her large family, including her son, daughter, brothers, sisters, cousins, nieces, and nephews. As a descendant of the Reverend John Robinson, the pastor to the Pilgrims, Dr. Petit loves to write about history, religious freedom, ancestry, dreams, reality, and our Lord and Savior, Jesus Christ. In addition to writing novels and poetry, Petit has been writing academic documents. She also has been a presenter at multiple libraries and academic conferences, including at the CCCC Conference in 2005 and at the NEWCA Conference in 2013. Some of this author's presentation topics are available on her author website: www.drkarenpetit.com.

Dr. Petit not only enjoys writing, but she also loves to help other people to write. For more than ten years, this author has been the full-time Writing Center Coordinator and an adjunct faculty member at the Community College of Rhode Island. Before starting full-time at this college, Petit worked as an adjunct faculty member for over twenty years at many area colleges: Bristol Community College, Massasoit Community College, Rhode Island College, Worcester State University, Quinsigamond Community College, Bryant University, Roger Williams University, New England Institute of Technology, the University of Massachusetts at Dartmouth, and the University of Rhode Island.

Dr. Karen Petit is very thankful for her amazing life. She has been enjoying her author events, as well as a large number of writing and educational activities. Her family, friends, and God have been the focus of her dreams, reality, and amazing holidays for many years.